GRANDAD SUPE

By Rob James

Illustrations by Matt James

MAPLE
PUBLISHERS

Grandad Supersub

Author: Rob James

Copyright © Rob James (2021)

Illustrations by Matt James

The right of Rob James to be identified as author of this work has been asserted by the author in accordance with section 77 and 78 of the Copyright, Designs and Patents Act 1988.

First Published in 2022

ISBN: 978-1-915164-87-2 (Paperback)

Book cover design and Book layout by:
　　White Magic Studios
　　www.whitemagicstudios.co.uk

Published by:
　　Maple Publishers
　　1 Brunel Way,
　　Slough,
　　SL1 1FQ, UK
　　www.maplepublishers.com

For our favourite footballers
Billy and Erin,
and for young at heart footballers everywhere.

Contents

KICK OFF

Chapter 1

At 77, Bert's grandad – also called Bert – was unusual.

There was nothing unusual about him being unusual because, unusually, he'd been unusual for a lot longer than Bert had been alive.

You see, Bert's grandad – also called Bert – was the world's oldest professional footballer.

And, what's more, he was still playing in the Premier League.

He had his age as his squad number and although he rarely completed a full 90 minutes, he was often brought on as a super-sub to win the game in the last few moments.

The fans loved him and told him so by singing 'We love you, grandad, we do' or 'Get your teeth out for the lads' whenever he came on.

In fact, when he scored a goal, he celebrated by taking his false teeth out, throwing them in the air and catching them in his mouth again.

You might think that Bert's grandad – also called Bert – would have been happy about this, and he was to a point.

But what was most unusual about Bert's grandad this season was that he had mentioned the 'r' word for the first time ever.

Now the 'r' word is 'retirement', and it means finishing work for good and taking it easy.

You see, Bert's grandad was a bit fed up. He hadn't been picked for England since he was 53 and his new club, Clegby Rovers, had refused to pay him in old money.

"You know, Bert" Bert's grandad would say to Bert's dad – also called Bert, "£20,000 a week just doesn't go as far these days as nine and eleven pence did in 1967."

He'd also been unhappy that Grandma had been photographed coming out of the post office still in her curlers and slippers, and the picture had appeared in all the papers.

And to add to it all, the Rovers manager who signed him had been sacked and new one, who was 65 years old, hired in his place.

Bert's grandad hated it when youngsters came in with their new-fangled ideas.

Oh, and there was the ball, which was too light, the boots, which were too comfy, and the shorts, which were not nearly long enough.

It's no wonder Bert's grandad felt like calling it a day.

He had had a long and distinguished career. He'd always played in the top division, never been relegated, and had played all over the world.

But Bert's grandad had never ever won a cup.

So, when Clegby Rovers made it through to the FA Cup final, Bert's grandad was as close as he had ever come to collecting a winner's medal and holding aloft the trophy.

But Bert's grandad was afraid he might be dropped for the final.

He had had to sit out the semi-final on the bench with his tartan blanket over his knees. The manager hadn't even asked him to warm up, so Bert's grandad sat there doing the crossword, waiting for the moment his team required their super-sub.

But it never came.

Even when the game was deep into injury time, the manager didn't tell him to take off his thermal tracksuit top and get ready for action.

The game finished 0-0, and finally Rovers went through 1-0 on penalties, even though each side had taken eighteen of them. They were to meet big-spending Richland City at Trembly Stadium in the final.

In the dressing room, while the Rovers players sprayed themselves with champagne and took turns throwing each other in the bath with their clothes still on, Bert's grandad packed his trusty leather kit bag – the only one he had ever had - and slipped out without a word.

Chapter 2

When he got home, Bert was there to meet him. He was so excited.

"Grandad, you're going to play in a cup final at last!" he exclaimed.

"I wouldn't be so sure," sighed Grandad. "The boss doesn't seem to think I'm worth picking."

"But you're the Rovers' super-sub. They're bound to need you for a cup final."

"Well," sighed Grandad, "I hope you're right. It certainly would be nice to finish with a cup and a shiny medal to keep."

Bert wondered what he could do to cheer Grandad up, or better still, make sure he was picked to play in the final.

But first, mum was taking Bert for a haircut.

Bert always insisted on going to Grandad's barber - Big Nige.

Big Nige the barber used to cut all the Rovers' players' hair, but now they went to the swanky salon over the road because they wanted something a bit different from short or very short, which were pretty much the choices at Nige's.

Just as Bert was having the hair around the ears trimmed, in burst a man with a Rovers scarf looking very concerned and sweaty.

"Does anyone know first aid?"

"Why?" said Nige, sounding bored, still snipping away. "What's happened now?"

"It's Jordan Gordan. He's hurt."

Now Jordan was Rovers' new star striker. He had cost fifty million pounds from Mansea Unispurs at the beginning of the season and was the England captain.

But as he had walked out of the swanky salon, his new floppy fringe extensions covered his designer sunglasses, a designer rip in his designer ripped jeans got caught on one of his girlfriend's designer shopping bags and he fell to the pavement, clutching his knee and rolling around in agony.

There was a big crowd around Jordan – or J-Dog, as some people insisted on calling him - and a lot of them were very worried Rovers fans.

"You see, Bert, that would never have happened to your

Grandad," said Nige.

"What do you mean?"

"Because he would have come in here for a smart trim to look his best for the cup final."

"Grandad thinks he won't be picked for the final," said Bert sadly.

"Well, he might just be in with a shout now this young whippersnapper's grazed his knee, or whatever it is he's done."

Bert ran home to tell Grandad the news, but grandad wasn't pleased.

"I don't want to get in the side just because somebody's hurt themselves," he said. "I want to be picked because I'm good enough to be picked, and right now I am not good enough to be picked."

He stormed off, but Bert whispered, "I think you are."

Chapter 3

The next day, Bert's grandad had just done 100 one-arm press-ups in training when the manager called him over.

"Jordan's out of the final," said the manager. "We might need you if things get desperate."

Bert's grandad felt insulted. "Desperate, eh? Why, I don't even think I'll bother getting on the coach to go to the game," he said to himself.

It was the morning of the final and Bert ran around to grandad's house to collect tickets for the family to watch the game.

Grandma answered the door.

"Hello, Gran," said Bert excitedly. "Did grandad leave the tickets for me and dad?"

"They're not the only things he left," said Gran.

Behind her stood Grandad, looking quite sad, but keeping a brave face.

"Grandad!" exclaimed Bert. "Shouldn't you be with the team going down to the final?"

"They don't really need me," said Grandad. "The manager said himself that he only wanted me to play if things got desperate. I don't want to be picked just because they're desperate."

"But grandad, you've always wanted to play in a cup final."

"I know, I know. But some things just aren't meant to be."

Just then the landline phone rang. Grandma answered it.

"Hello – yes, he's here." She said then told Grandad. "It's the manager. He wants to know why you're not on the coach."

"Tell him I don't want to play just because they're desperate."

"You tell him," said Grandma sternly.

Grandad reached for the receiver, but Bert got there ahead of him.

"My grandad's never played in a cup final and it's the one thing he wanted to do before he retired but you told him he could only play if you were desperate and he's very sad and thinks he's not good enough anymore but I think he is and so do lots and lots and lots of other people and if you think he is then you will come and pick us up at 33 Cumbersome Road. RIGHT NOW!"

...he squeaked and slammed the phone down, and burst into floods of tears.

"Oh, Grandad," said Bert. "It wasn't just about you playing in the cup final, it was about us seeing you there. It didn't matter whether you played or not. You're always the best footballer in the world to us."

Now Grandad was in tears.

"Well," he said. "I can't not go now, can I? Unless the coach doesn't turn up, of course."

They waited for a few anxious minutes to see if the huge, air-conditioned coach – complete with jacuzzi and table-tennis table – came around the corner.

After what seemed like forever, it did.

The coach stopped outside the house and the door ssshhhhhhhhhed open.

The manager stepped down. He looked as though he was in shock.

"Come on, Bert," he said. "I'm sorry I said we'd need you if we were desperate. I didn't mean it to sound like that."

Bert's grandad – who was also called Bert, remember – picked up his leather kit bag.

He turned to Bert and Grandma and said, "Come on, then you two."

Then he said to Bert, "We'll pick your mum and dad up on the way."

Dad was very surprised to see the team coach pull up outside the house but pleased because that meant he didn't have to "faff around trying to get parked", as he put it.

The five of them sat at the front of the coach as it headed down the motorway.

Chapter 4

Bert couldn't believe he was on the footballers' coach.

He gazed open-mouthed at the players all the way to the final.

They all had dark blue blazers and ties, and matching headphones. Some were playing cards. Others were talking or watching videos on their phones. One was even reading a book.

There was a lot of laughing and joking, but some looked nervous and quiet – the manager most of all.

Bert's grandad did the crossword and sucked mint humbugs – he didn't have his own teeth, so it didn't matter - while Grandma did lots of Sudoku puzzles very quickly.

His dad flapped about where he'd put his tickets and chatted with the driver about favourite football matches and nightmare coach journeys (Bert's dad hated flying so he'd been on many coach holidays and excursions).

Bert's mum read a magazine with stories like 'My brother tried to sell my leg' or 'I loved him, but he smelled of fish'.

When they arrived at the stadium, the players kindly let Bert and his family get off first so they could find their seats.

Grandad said goodbye to Bert, Bert's dad, Bert's mum and kissed Grandma, and then picked up his leather kit bag and headed for the changing rooms.

First the team had to inspect the pitch and talk to the TV reporters. All of them wanted to talk to Bert's grandad.

"Is it true it's your last game?" they asked. Bert's grandad said he hoped it would be, although he secretly thought he had already played his last game.

"What will you do when you retire?" enquired another reporter.

"I think I'll take up rugby," said Bert's grandad. "Or ride the Tour de France."

The teams went back inside to get changed.

While the Rovers team were getting changed, J-Dog hobbled in on his crutches to wish them luck and hobbled out again.

Just then, grandad wandered outside to go and speak to the referee, as he always liked to introduce himself and say "Enjoy the game, ref." as he thought that was good manners.

As he walked across the corridor, he heard a voice say, "Can I just say what an excellent choice you've made, Jordan? Don't worry about missing this cup final. There'll be lots of finals for you when you play for us. This time next week you'll be a Richland player."

Grandad tiptoed to the end of the corridor and peered around the corner.

There was Jordan Gordan and his agent shaking hands with the chairman of Richland City, although the agent was saying that they still had to "talk proper money."

'Well, well,' he thought. 'I thought I'd seen it all, but this takes the biscuit.'

He turned away and went in to see the referee.

The linesmen were arguing about whose black shorts were whose and whose black socks were whose, and the neither could remember which of them was supposed to have the red or yellow flag.

The referee blew his whistle very loudly and they stopped arguing and put their hands over their ears.

"Just came to say enjoy the game, ref," said Bert's grandad.

"That's very kind of you, Bert," said the ref. "I don't think I need to tell you about not using foul and abusive language, do I?"

"I don't think I know any," joked Bert's grandad. The referee smiled and the linesmen started bickering again.

Back in the changing room, the manager had started talking tactics with the help of a huge interactive video screen on which he could move his players around. Bert's grandad never listened to the tactics.

"If you're good enough, you know where to be and when to be there", he always said.

But he knew where he was going to be at the start of the game, anyway – on the bench.

And he was right.

But first, he would walk through the tunnel and into the stadium with the barely believable noise of 100,000 supporters ringing in his ears.

Or at least he would have a few years ago, but he was a bit deaf these days.

The colours of Rovers at one end of the stadium and Richland City at the other made for an incredible sight.

Streamers, toilet rolls and balloons floated down on to the pitch, which made Bert's grandad 'tut' because he hated litter.

Once they reached the pitch, Bert's grandad would line up with his team mates and meet the Prime Minister, who was guest of honour at the final. Bert's grandad had hoped to meet the Queen.

The Prime Minister shook each of the players by the hand and simply said things like: "Love footie, me. Big fan. Big fan."

But Bert's grandad, who had a proper good old-fashioned handshake which made your fingers go white and numb, wanted a word about a few things.

So, he went on about there not being enough for young people to do with their spare time and the closure of the last mint humbug making factory in the country until the Prime Minister's eyes were watering from the pain of the handshake and he was unable to speak because he was gritting his teeth so hard.

Once Bert's grandad had finished and the chairman of the Football Association had rescued the Prime Minister, he had to use his other hand to greet the rest of the players.

Once that was over, Bert's grandad took his place on the bench and the game began.

Chapter 5

It wasn't a classic cup final.

There were no goals by half time. In fact, there were no goals at full time, and that meant extra time.

Bert's grandad couldn't remember whether or not he'd slept through some of the game, not that he'd missed anything. He spent most of the time wondering how he could get his lawn to look as good as the Trembly pitch.

The manager got the players together and gave them yet another team talk.

He brought on two substitutes, but not Bert's grandad, who walked back to his spot on the bench.

As he did so, he looked up into the stands and there he could just see Bert, Bert's mum and dad and Grandma – but only if he squinted.

Bert was waving furiously, and Bert's grandad waved back.

No sooner had he sat down and put his trusty tartan blanket over his legs – even though it was a lovely warm May day – than the whistle blew and the crowd went bananas.

The referee had awarded a penalty to Richland City.

What's more, the Rovers keeper was out cold. The physio was talking into his radio mic and making a funny bent arms moving up and down sign, which meant they needed a stretcher, and his assistant was making a rolling movement with his hands to tell the manager that they needed a substitute.

But the manager was in shock. He hadn't picked a substitute goalkeeper. He didn't know what to do.

So, when Bert's grandad, a marauding centre forward who'd always loved mucking around in goal in training, neatly folded up his blanket and put a bookmark in the spy novel he had brought along to make sure he wouldn't lose his page, said, "I'll have a go," the manager grabbed a green shirt and thrust it into Bert's grandad's hands.

Bert's grandad took off his thermal tracksuit top and his Rovers outfield shirt to reveal his lucky string vest.

He pulled on the keeper's jersey.

The kit man handed him some very fancy, ergonomically designed, super-grip gloves.

But Bert's grandad smiled and said: "I don't need them, son."

He took his time getting to the penalty area where Richland's Uruguayan star striker Eugene Eugenio was standing waiting to burst the net with his penalty.

The Rovers captain, Darren Beckston, was waiting for Bert's grandad.

"He nearly always shoots to the keeper's left," he said in between big, gasping breaths. "But sometimes goes to the right and sometimes down the middle. Sometimes they are high and sometimes they are low."

"Very helpful," said Bert's grandad. "Thank you."

Eugenio stood looking at the ball. The referee was busy making sure Bert's grandad was on his line.

"Wait for my whistle," he said.

The whistle blew.

Eugenio started his run-up. He took one step and pretended to stop, took another step, and did a rather curious crouching movement before another pretend stop and then one more step before smacking the ball low and hard to Bert's grandad's right.

Now, Bert's grandad could never understand goalkeepers who dived before the kick had been taken, so he left his dive to the last possible nanosecond.

But, as he didn't so much fly as tumble to his right, he realised that the penalty was going to be just beyond his fingertips.

There was only one thing to do. Quick as a flash, he spat out his false teeth and they went pinging into the ball, diverting it on to the post and away to the feet of a Rovers defender who hacked it into the furthest tier of Trembly Stadium.

The Rovers fans went berserk and the players were mobbing Bert's grandad and kissing him on the cheeks, which he wasn't keen on at all – a good firm handshake and a "well done, old chap" was much more his style. Besides, he couldn't find his teeth with all the cuddling that was going on.

The City players, meanwhile, were chasing after the referee who was doing that very fast running backwards that only referees can do. They were protesting that it wasn't allowed, that it was cheating, or that having false teeth gave Bert's grandad an unfair advantage and that they would take this to the FA, UEFA, FIFA and the United Nations if they couldn't take the penalty again.

But all they got was ten yellow cards between them, and the referee waved play on.

Chapter 6

For the next 28 minutes, the players got more and more tired and more and more rubbish. Their passes went to the wrong players and their shots just dribbled towards the goals.

Bert's grandad didn't have another save to make.

Just as the game entered the last few seconds before it would go to penalties, Bert's grandad sent an almighty punt down the pitch.

And then he ran.

His exhausted team mates looked in astonishment at the old man sprinting down the pitch after his own kick.

The City players were equally bewildered, so much so that when one tried to trap the ball, he slipped and sent the ball straight into the path of the aged striker.

Bert's grandad beat one tired defender, then another and then a third.

He had reached the edge of the area and there was only the keeper to beat. But Bert's grandad was so tired himself by now he could barely run another step.

There was only one thing for it - Bert's Banana.

It was a shot that Bert's grandad had perfected in the 1950s when he played against the likes of Stanley Matthews and Tom Finney.

You hit the ball with the outside of your foot and it would curl wickedly around the keeper and into the net.

'Here goes,' he thought. He struck it sweetly and the ball flew around the City keeper, who was rooted to the spot, gobsmacked because he had never seen a ball swerve so much.

It seemed to be bound for the top corner when - 'SMACK' – it hit the post and shook the goal.

The ball bounced across the goal line and then hit the other post and swerved back towards the City keeper.

But of course, these balls aren't like the ones Bert's grandad learned to do Bert's Banana with. The old ones were as hard as a rhino's bum and weighed as much as a cannonball when they were wet.

This one, on the other hand, was so silky smooth and ultra-light and that with the help of the Bert's Banana Super Spin it twirled in all directions. The keeper twisted awkwardly to make his save, but it slipped like a wriggly eel through his hands and trickled over the line.

The referee's watch buzzed to tell him it had crossed the line and he blew to award the goal. Just as the goalkeeper wearily retrieved the ball from the back of the net, the referee blew his whistle again.

It was the final whistle and there was pandemonium inside Trembly Stadium, and in pubs and living rooms up and down the country.

Bert's grandad had won the cup for Clegby Rovers in his very first cup final and his very last match.

Bert, Bert's mum and dad and Grandma hugged and kissed each other. The Rovers players hugged and kissed each other, although they shook Bert's grandad's hand, which they all regretted.

The manager was doing a little dance in the middle of the pitch, which was covered in bits of paper that Bert's grandad was feverishly picking up, 'tutting' as he did so. People wanted to pat him on the back, but Bert's grandad just wanted to find a bin to put all the rubbish in.

The Richland players were sitting on the grass. Some were crying, others were staring into space.

When things had died down a bit, the teams went up to get their medals and Rovers collected the cup. In fact, Bert's grandad was given the honour of lifting the cup, although there was an embarrassing moment when the Prime Minister wasn't too sure about another handshake.

The fans ran onto the pitch and Bert's grandad was carried around on their shoulders with the cup held high in the air.

"Just like Stanley Matthews," he thought.

Chapter 7

Back in the changing rooms, the manager was all smiles and glowing about Bert's grandad. It was as if the word 'desperate' had never passed his lips.

Then in came Jordan Gordan.

"Fantastic, lads. I knew you could do it. We are the cup winners!" A massive cheer went up and there was a popping of champagne corks.

Bert's grandad just smiled. He didn't want to make a fuss. He got dressed and packed his leather kit bag for the last time and went to meet Bert and the family.

As he walked towards the door, he stopped, leaned towards Jordan, and said, "Don't worry, son. I'm sure there'll be plenty of cup finals for you….just like the man said."

No one else heard. They didn't have to. But Jordan knew that Bert's grandad knew, and he felt a bit sick. He quietly hobbled out of the changing room, down the corridor and out of sight.

Bert was so excited to see his grandad, he could barely speak. The press swarmed around Bert's grandad wanting quotes and pictures and they all voted him man-of-the-match on all their websites, even though he'd only played for thirty minutes.

"Why on earth did he think of using his false teeth?" they asked.

"Well," he said, "the balls these days, they're so light that it doesn't take much to deflect them, so I reckoned it was worth a go."

"In the old days, I wouldn't have dared. The balls then would have smashed my teeth to smithereens. I'm very sorry for spitting, though. That's never very nice to see."

Going back on the coach, Bert said, "I don't want to be a footballer."

"Why on earth not?" asked grandad.

"EH?!!' exclaimed dad.

"Because you have to wait until you're 77 to be the best footballer ever – and I don't think I can wait that long."

Back home, Bert's grandad put his medal in a little display case on the mantelpiece.

"Nice, isn't it?" he said to Grandma.

"Very shiny," she said, "Now will you promise me there'll be no more football?"

"I promise," he said.

But he had his fingers crossed behind his back....

FULL TIME